The
Adventures
of Anybody

The Adventures of Anybody

Richard Bandler

Meta Publications Inc.
P.O. Box 1910, Capitola, CA 95010
(831) 464-0254 Fax (831) 464-0517
www.meta-publications.com

Printed in the United States of America.

Library of Congress Card Number 93-084506
ISBN 0-916990-29-X

Table of Contents

Foreword

"Through hearts of stone and will of vile mush
we all weave our life. Until passion's fire joins
with light of love to melt and boil away fools
and brutes… or else my children… you just fade

away"

a way

a way

I began writing this tale in 1975 after writing five books in less than two years, all quote, non fiction. The Adventures of Anybody —Tales of Meta for You was my escape, my passion, my chance to take what I had learned building models of language and unconscious and unconsciously put it to use. However, journeys are never as easy as they appear if they are to be worthwhile. My journey twisted through many people and places and lead to see all change comes to be the right direction when the heart grows tired of the mind not the reverse. So I dedicate this book first to all the illusions along the way. Hopefully their journey will lead them to something more worthwhile. I dedicate this volume mostly to a heart that with mind knows passion can grow beyond what we would never suspect. Remember life gets better when you're headed in the right direction and you'll know it's right because you're sure enough to be unsure about but never unsure enough to not do it.

Very, very dedicated…

So to my friend, companion, and fountain of passion I dedicate this to you
Paula Mae Bandler. We are.

With love that is building
not just anybody in particular
we are
beyond time……

efore we begin I must state that what we are presenting here is nothing more than a fable. A fable is just one way to let your imagination run away with you—now—so, figuratively speaking, just imagine you were this poor young prince right here in the middle of somewhere, and that you longed for a new experience. When you were young everything was always new—new toys, new games, new sports, riding and hunting and such. But now everything was old. Hunting was old, the castle was old, even his friends were getting old.

So he went to the court jester and commanded him: "Make me laugh." The court jester just performed the same old tricks and the same old jokes. "Uhmmm," thought the Prince. "How could so much nothing be right here in the middle of somewhere?" So the Prince decided that perhaps he had not looked far enough; he must try harder.

He next went to the court scholar and commanded him to teach him something new. The scholar began to teach him history, but the Prince complained that history was just old-now. The scholar began to teach him advanced mathematics but the Prince complained it was just a new way of doing old things.

The court scholar became concerned, as scholars should. He told the King that it wasn't right for someone not to want to learn old things, to do old things. The scholar exclaimed, "If everybody was always doing new things, we'd have chaos. No one would know what to expect from anybody. We would all be in a constant state of surprise and thus two things would surely happen. First we would all be worn out from the excitement of it all and the neighboring kingdom would launch a surprise attack that we wouldn't expect because we were so used to surprise we wouldn't plan for it. It's happened many times before in history. Believe me, it's nothing new. And second, if we were always surprised we would get so used to it that we wouldn't notice it anyway. So," declared the scholar, "the boy has a problem beyond my help. The court physician will surely have to be called in."

At all this fuss the Prince was somewhat confused. On the one hand he felt bad about the concerned face of the King and all the disappointed faces of the elders of the court as they muttered, "What can we do? What a terrible thing to happen to the King; he was so proud. How will his mother take it?" On the other hand, all this was something new.

The court physician was called at once. He checked the Prince's tongue and eyes, his nose and ears. In fact, he searched from toe to head but he could not find one thing wrong with the Prince. So he concluded, "The trouble must be on the inside, so we will have to put something on the inside to fix it."

So numerous potions and teas and mixtures were given to the Prince. But he would only triumphantly exclaim that since he had a new problem, old potions and formulas would not affect it. The Prince would then roar with laughter and delight at the newness of it all. This concerned the court physician more than ever. He would raise an eyebrow and say to the King, "His symptoms are getting worse."

The King was so worried he didn't know what to do or where to turn, so he convened the whole court and offered a great reward for anyone who could cure his son, the Prince. He also secretly convened the Captain of the Guards and all his generals and told them to beware, that this might be a plot to overthrow the kingdom and there could be no telling how long before other people in the kingdom might want something new.

Suddenly spies were everywhere, watching and listening, trying to discover who gave the Prince this problem in the first place. All the physicians in

the land worked day and night to cure the Prince. But the problem was not so dried and cut.

The Prince meanwhile was becoming very nervous; he now knew that he had a problem that no one could solve. He became scared and worried and would whimper for hours, wishing this terrible thing had not befallen him. "Why not somebody else? Why me?" The court physician only raised his eyebrow high and said to the King, "His symptoms are getting worse." They bled him and prayed for him but all were at a loss.

Finally, in desperation, the King yelled to all his wise servants of the court, "If you cannot think of anything else to help my son I shall cut off all your heads." The scholars, physicians, and advisors of the court were very afraid, so they finally went to the King and solemnly they said, "There is only one more thing we can think of for the King to do to help his son."

"What is it?" demanded the King.

"Get the sorcerer who roams the deserts to the south."

The King proclaimed, "Bring this man to me."

"We cannot," answered the wise men of court. "The King must request him to come, no man or warrior can subdue him. He is a mesmerizer and can put spells upon any number of men. This is why we did not tell you about him before. He is dangerous and might put a spell on the King or the Prince."

The King looked back at his advisors with a furrowed brow. He said, "I am old, and no one else can help my son. I must then meet this sorcerer and take my chances with one who casts spells."

The request was sent to the sorcerer. The King waited the whole first day, the whole second day, the whole third day, the whole fourth day, the whole fifth day, the whole sixth day, the whole seventh day, the whole eighth day, the whole ninth day, and on the tenth day he grew so impatient that he called the Court together and demanded an explanation.

The wise men decided the King would have to tempt the sorcerer with gold and riches. An offer was sent, and ten more days passed while the King continued to worry and the Prince sank deeper and deeper into gloom. And so the King sent another offer to the sorcerer. He said he would give to the sorcerer anything within his power if he would cure his son.

And so at last the sorcerer came to the palace. When he came to the Prince, the Prince was very surprised because he expected the sorcerer to be dressed in robes of black with a pointed hat with stars on it. The sorcerer was not dressed this way at all; he wore robes of royal purple and had no hat at all. His hair was white as snow and avalanched down his back and shoulders and through his bushy eyebrows gleamed two bright lights. The Prince could not detect their color. They seemed to change from brown to blue, then to hazel, then to brown.

The King begged the sorcerer, "Please cure my son." The sorcerer smiled a queer smile and slowly he began to speak. "My dear King, I do not have to cure your son because your son, the Prince, has no problem at all. In fact, there is no Prince at all, all this is just part of a dream someone is having somewhere who does not know he is really dreaming, and a problem in a dream is no real problem at all."

All the Court agreed that this made good sense and the King sighed with relief. However, the Prince became worried because if the dreaming is going on somewhere, then here isn't somewhere and so here must be nowhere. And for a moment the Prince became confused about whether he was really in somewhere, or nowhere, or in fact whether he was anywhere at all.

In this process he even forgot that he was a Prince and the world began to spin—or was it the dream that was spinning? He couldn't quite figure out which. In all the spinning he must have fallen asleep, or woken up. (He wasn't quite sure.) But he was sure that he was not in the King's castle. In fact he was pretty sure he was not in any of the King's lands because he had never seen this place before, at least he was as sure as anyone can be of anything in such circumstances. And he asked himself, "I wonder where I am. In fact, I wonder if I am awake or asleep."

With this he decided he would explore and put off such an important decision until later. And so he stopped worrying about where he was and who he was and began to explore to find out what could be found out. And he found this a strange place indeed.

ow Anybody Got His Name

One of the things that stops a fable from being a story is that there is not even one shred of truth in it. And, as everyone knows, fables must be short and stories, even short ones, must be longer. Also we must keep in mind that even if stories can be almost as short as fables, a story can never be as deep.

The Prince who, through some trouble we do not need to discuss further, has forgotten he is a Prince, [in fact he never really was.] And this poor young chap is somewhere, although he is not quite sure where.

This place has some rather peculiar characteristics. Imagine that you had to deal with such an impossible actuality as finding yourself in the middle of a green field. And though you can't remember, you have always believed in the right things and felt you were basically a sane person. Though you were not always perfect, you never believed in make-believe, yet, here right in front of you, in a green field, you were face to face with a small little man. Though he was smaller than you, he did look older, and as he got up off a rock on which he was sitting, he got larger and younger.

The young Prince who had forgotten that he was a Prince shook his head and looked in amazement at the approaching little man, who walked up and grew up and got younger all at the same time. The strange little man said, "My name is Blink. What is your name?"

The reply was silence from an opened mouth. The Prince began to answer as any polite person would, but to his amazement no words came out. The strange little man cocked his head and furrowed his eyebrows in concern. "Can you speak louder?" he said. "I cannot hear you."

"That is because I did not say anything," the Prince replied.

The little man nodded in understanding.

"I do not know my name, in fact I do not know where I am or even what time it is."

The strange little man began to scratch his head. "That doesn't make any sense. You have to be somebody and surely you are here; as for time, what does time mean?"

The Prince suddenly thought all this wasn't funny and scornfully replied, "Of course, I'm here, but where is here compared with where I should be, and it is not that I am not somebody, it is just that I don't know who. I have only forgotten who I am. I must be somebody..."

The little man, who all at once seemed quite relieved, blurted out, "Well, if you're somebody, why didn't you just say so? Glad to make your acquaintance. Somebody, perhaps I can help you find your way if you're lost." The little man began to ramble on and on about thousands of roads, their names and destinations, none of which had any meaning to somebody lost in the way the Prince was. So the Prince just dropped down on the ground and began to cry and whimper that nobody understood him and he had lost his identity.

With this, Blink interrupted and empathetically declared that if this was a case of lost identity they would just have to go to the police. So Somebody and Blink went to the nearest police station, which was at the edge of the forest in which the green field had decided to exist.

Upon entering the police station, Blink greeted the sergeant with polite amenities and then apologized for not introducing the somebody who was with him. But as he explained to the sergeant, "You see, this is the very problem with which we need your help. My friend here has lost his identity."

The sergeant nodded know-
ingly and murmured under
his breath, "Lost his identity, ahhhn." The sergeant
turned to Somebody and
suspiciously looked him
over, then inquired, "You
sure that it wasn't stolen?"

"I'm quite sure," Somebody
replied.

"Do you know how you lost
it?"

"I do not."

"Then," the sergeant ex-
claimed with resolution,
"you don't know for sure
that it wasn't stolen."

"I guess I don't."

"Well then," said the sergeant as he drew out the appropriate forms, "this
sounds like a case of robbery to me. An identity is too important a thing

to lose, so it must have been stolen. Robbery I'd say, sure as I'm alive." Blink seemed to be in full agreement with the sergeant, so finally Somebody agreed that it was robbery.

The sergeant assured him that everything that had ever been stolen in his district had been returned and so as soon as the proper forms were filled out, the case was as good as closed.

The sergeant murmured under his breath, "Robbery, date, uhmmm, let's see, name please?"

"I have no name—it was taken with my identity."

"No name!" the sergeant cried. "How will I fill out the forms?"

Blink, who was by nature a helpful person, told the sergeant it was no problem to just fill in "unknown" and let it go at that. The sergeant agreed that this was acceptable. "Your address?"

"Unknown."

"Time of robbery?"

"Unknown."

"Place of crime?"

"Unknown."

The sergeant became very flustered and, shaking his head back and forth, said, "I don't have a case without a file, and a file that has no information is no file at all, a crime must be committed on someone somewhere at some time or it is no crime at all. So though I would like to help you, I think this is a matter for higher authorities. So I will just have to escort you to the district judge; he is wise and knows how to consider facts. He will surely be able to help you."

The journey to the courthouse was long and uneventful. The sergeant presented Somebody and Blink to the judge who was very, very old. His face was stern and he made no expression as the sergeant presented the problem. He was as old as time itself and twice as wise. Blink assured Somebody that the judge would surely have the solution. He never failed to have a solution.

After the whole problem had been described the judge sighed and shook his head as if he had heard this whole thing a thousand times before. He looked down sternly, as a tired father would to any child who asked a silly question. "Listen," said the judge, "and listen to me well so that this problem is never brought before my bench again.

"Obviously this poor fellow has either lost or had his identity stolen—that could happen to anybody, so until he recovers what is rightfully his, he is Anybody. So now you have a name for your silly forms. And listen to

me, young man. Don't tell people you don't know who you are or that you're just somebody. We have firmly established that you are Anybody.

"As for recovering what is yours, that is a simple matter. You have lost your identity; an identity is like anything else that people wear for years. It has a particular fit, so I suggest that you go around and try on all the identities in the district until you find the one that fits. That one will be your own and the person who is wearing it will be the culprit."

It all seemed so simple now. They just couldn't imagine how they had failed to see what was so obvious. They all thanked the judge and set out together to find an identity that would fit Anybody.

Anybody was much relieved to have at least a partial solution to his problem, but he wondered, "Who could I be?" He asked Blink, "Who do you think I'll find out that I am?"

Blink looked at him from head to toe. "Well, you're too young to be the judge and if you were him, we would have had to consult you for the solution to your problem, so I believe the judge is out. I'm really quite sure that you're not me because you're much too tall and your eyes are the wrong color. You don't look much like a policeman; you don't look like a blacksmith because your arms are too small. No, you don't look like anybody specific I know. You look sort of general, you could be anybody."

"I am Anybody," Anybody protested. "Now I want to be somebody in particular."

"Oh," said Blink. "I can understand that. I think you should try being a few people and maybe that would give you an idea of who you would like to be."

"Don't be silly," said Anybody. "Nobody gets to be who they would like to be. It's just unheard of. You have to be somebody else so that you can want to be the person you want to be. If you were the person you wanted to be then you wouldn't want to be that person so I must be somebody else."

Blink agreed with this and was so impressed he decided that surely Anybody must be somebody intelligent. And so they set out to try on the identity of each of the local scholarly men.

They walked for half a day until they reached a think forest. Blink said the wisest men of all resided in this forest, because in the middle of a place so twisted with vines and thickets the average man would get lost. It is the place where a man of higher education is most at home. Blink went on to explain that the local preoccupation was to know every twist and turn of every bush so you could predict just what route any stranger would take on any given day given the starting point and of course the destination.

Anybody might have asked about the point of such doings, but he assumed that anything he couldn't understand how to use must be very important indeed. So instead he asked Blink, "What is my destination?" Blink only shrugged his shoulders and said, "I don't know my way around, so we must just walk around a little until we find someone who might be you."

They entered the forest. Although they could see very little, they felt their way along until a voice shouted in a contemptuous tone, "How dare you walk around blindly? You can't just have taken the course you have. Where is your destination?" Anybody, much taken aback, decided whoever this person was, he surely could not be Anybody. He thought to himself, "I am much too polite for such discourteousness."

The stranger shouted again, almost in complete anger, "I say, where is your destination?" Blink replied, "We have none."

"Poppycock," said the voice. "Everybody has a direction. Since you are part of the set of somebody you must have a direction or you would not be here going or coming. You see, it is simple logic."

Anybody felt confused at this but assured the voice that he was Anybody and had come with Blink into this forest not to go or come but rather to find, and since he did not know who he was looking for he did not know where he was and so he could have no direction.

The voice yelled, "Bravo, bravo, I am delighted to meet a man so versed in the discipline of thought." A man of great height stepped out from behind a tree and extended his hand in welcome. "Are you of the Letters?" he inquired while he shook Anybody's hand in friendship. Anybody replied, "I might be, kind sir (though he really was thinking how unkind the stranger had been). I have lost my identity and I am looking for the man who has it. I just thought it might be in this forest." The stranger stopped shaking Anybody's hand and said, "Perhaps I can assist you. I have seen many identities worn through by many people who come and go in this forest. Who were you?"

Anybody might have said, "I don't know." But he was tired of saying that he had no name that he could remember. Besides, he knew with total conviction that he was, at least for the time, Anybody. So he replied, "I am just Anybody."

The old scholar leaned over to Anybody and gazed at him keenly. He asked inquisitively, "Is that your name really?"

Anybody could have replied by recounting the whole set of circumstances, but he was content to say only that at this time it was his real name and at some other it was someone else's. The old scholar thought this over and began again. "How can I be of service to you? It's not everyday that Anybody comes by." The old man began to laugh to himself and repeat his words over and over.

Anybody got very mad and told the scholar his problem as far as he and Blink could tell it. The scholar apologized for his not understanding the seriousness of the situation. He then suggested that they consult other scholars since the problem was really an academic one by nature.

So the old man led them through the forest, and told them that there was a clearing in the middle of the forest where the oldest tree in the land grew. There he would summon the wise men and together their great minds would find the solution.

On the way through the forest Anybody asked the wise old man why men of knowledge lived in the old forest. He recounted the explanation given to him by Blink and asked for the truth of the matter. The old scholar, with dignity and sincerity, simply stated, "What was in the forest was understood and predictable to those acquainted with it. What was on the outside of the forest was unexplainable in terms of the forest. So as all educated men do when something is unexplainable, they let religion explain it. Religion was very good for explaining what was not in the forest, but it was not much use in the forest so we left it out and ourselves in." All this made almost no sense to Anybody, but he acted as if he understood completely.

Soon Anybody was sitting on the ground in a clearing in the middle of the forest with a gnarled and withered tree standing before him. He was surrounded by old scholars from every part of the forest: men old and young with white hair and brown, and every imaginable type of dress and manner of speaking. They were discussing the problems of Anybody, trying like the wise men they were to find a logical solution. Anybody just grew tired and hungry and finally so sleepy that he leaned up against Blink and went to sleep.

The second thing that he became aware of as he awoke was the distant, muted tinkling of what sounded like thousands and thousands of tiny bells. This sound so intrigued him that he quite comfortably forgot what the first thing had been.

As he eagerly drew himself to his feet, he noticed that in the snug grass in the little hollow under the towering tree where he had been sleeping there was the outline of not one form but two. Beside himself with both alarm and curiosity, he glanced rapidly around him, hoping to discover someone else. Upon seeing no one, he stretched himself like a cat and was pleasantly surprised to find that he was dressed from head to toe in a warm, smooth, lightweight green jump suit—the fabric was wholly unlike fabrics he had experienced before.

The sun reflected brilliantly off the dew, which still sparkled on the blades of grass in the field that bordered the edge of the forest. As he strode into the sunlight, he felt strength flowing through his entire body, refreshing him. He wanted very much to discover the source of the tinkling sounds, which still filled the air from time to time. So, taking the first path that led in the direction of those sounds, he walked on for a great distance.

He was just beginning to wonder where he was and when he would meet someone when he saw a trail of smoke rising above the trees into which the path he was following disappeared. As he entered the woods, he could smell the fire. As the tinkling sound had stopped, he was also able to hear the sound of rushing water.

A short distance into the woods, he came upon a cottage beside a stream. Delighted, he quickened his pace and, reaching the door, he knocked. The door swung open slowly, and in the shaft of light that penetrated the cottage he could see only the most amazing rug he had ever seen. Directly in the center of the portion of the rug lighted by the sunshine was a huge, smooth, round ball of crystal whose diameter was nearly equal to his height.

No sound came from the interior of the cottage. After calling out several times in hopes of attracting the attention of the cottage's owner, he stepped inside and firmly closed the door. The very second that the man set foot inside the cottage, even as he was closing the door, a tremendous ringing of thousands and thousands of tiny bells began. With the door closed the sound of the bells receded to a distant murmur and, although he could not discover its source, the entire interior of the cottage was softly lit.

The thought—low and melodious—came to him: "EAT." Glancing around the cottage, he noticed a steaming bowl of some sort of porridge, a goblet full of a golden liquid that smelled like fresh apricots, butter and several slices of rich dark bread that, to his surprise, was warm to the touch.

Well, he thought to himself, I may as well eat. I shall need strength, whatever happens next in this adventure.

No sooner had he finished his meal when the silverware and dishes gave off a high pitch and three flashes of light and vanished without a trace of sound. At the same instant, a low-pitched, gently wavering melodious voice filled his mind and the cottage. At first the words were indistinct, although he knew their meaning. Then the words became distinct and he wandered in front of the faintly gleaming ball of crystal.

"Settle yourself comfortably all the way down."

A comfortable chair-couch appeared beneath him, and he did.

"I am ready to answer your questions—ask them." The voice enveloped him and he thought he saw flashes of light in the globe. He was breathing comfortably. His hands rested lightly on his thighs.

"Who are you?"

"And who are you?" the voice replied.

"I'm Anybody," he replied with confidence.

"How do you know that you are Anybody?"

"And how do I know that I'm Anybody?" he asked himself. And he wondered what it would be like to not be anybody. "I'm not sure," he answered finally.

"Do you really think that because you're not sure you're Anybody?"

This confused him at first. "No, I mean, I don't know how I know I'm Anybody."

"Would you like to learn how to really be Anybody?" the voice coaxed gently.

"What do you mean?" He felt somewhat alarmed at this question.

"I mean learning how to really be Anybody," the voice answered with a soft chuckle.

As the voice faded away, his eyes focused on the swirling mists within the ball of crystal and Anybody again smelled the sweet cool morning air even as he had this very morning. The singing of a bird and the sound of air rushing through the leaves of a tree were overhead. The mists slowly parted and he saw the figure of a young man dressed in green from head to toe. The man began to stir, and just as he was opening his eyes, he heard the sound, distant and muted, of many bells.

Anybody could feel his heartbeat quicken. He leaned slightly forward in his chair-couch. The young man shortly rose to his feet and glanced back to where he had been lying, looked around with quick movements, then stretched and, after a short pause, moved across a field.

Anybody continued to watch and listen to what happened to the young man in the ball of crystal but his attention wandered. His body was tensed as if to avoid something, so he deliberately smoothed and deepened his breathing. The sounds, smells, and sights that came to him from the ball of crystal were strangely familiar, and they could sometimes ring a bell inside Anybody. His body jerked slightly as if to demand his full attention to what was occurring before him. He heard the sound of rushing water. There was smoke and the events in the ball seemed to accelerate. A knocking on a door startled him so that he nearly jumped out of his chair-couch.

He heard an indistinct cry from both within the ball of crystal and without. It sounded like someone calling, "Is Anybody home? Is Anybody home?"

The mists swirled all about within the ball. He allowed his head to fall back against the high back of the chair-couch, and knew no more.

When Anybody regained consciousness, the young man was just finishing eating. Anybody shivered slightly when he heard three high-pitched bursts of sound followed by a low, melodious murmuring and saw the young man slowly turn and move toward him for the reflection in the ball of crystal. He froze with alarm as the figure appeared to step into his very shoes, turn and then lower himself into the very chair-couch that Anybody was sitting in. And then he understood.

The voice began to laugh softly but the laughter grew to gale-like proportions, almost shaking him. He thought his mind would split.

He became aware that the laughter had stopped.

"Well, do you understand how to really be Anybody?" the voice asked quietly.

"No, I don't understand."

His mind was in turmoil. He wondered what would happen next. "And you wonder what will happen next, don't you?"

Anybody could not at that. And he did. He came to his senses when he caught the first wafts of the sweet, cool morning air. The second thing that he became aware of was the distant, muted tinkling of what sounded like thousands and thousands of tiny bells. He drew himself to his feet under the towering tree automatically, his mind racing ahead to find some way of breaking the inevitable flow of events.

He struggled desperately. He knew exactly what would happen unless he was able to act. As he approached the woods where the sound of rushing water and the smell of smoke emerged from, his breathing changed, becoming harsh. He noticed his hands were clenched into fists. His vision was blurred and there seemed to be a faint luminosity coming from the right, near where the path entered the woods. As he drew abreast of it, he hurled himself with all his strength right toward where he had glimpsed the glowing.

Time seemed suspended. He moved his body as though through a thick viscous fluid. His body felt heavy and unresponsive. There was a slight whispering in his ears. The pressure grew as he noticed his feet passing over the edge of the road. Suddenly, as though his body had been attached to a gigantic rubber band that had snapped, he shot forward at such a high rate of speed he stumbled and fell, his momentum sending his body rolling through the high green grass for some distance.

He saw a huge, many-legged creature with antennae moving through an interminable forest of bending and swaying plants and he smelled dark, rich earth. He wondered why he felt no alarm at the approach of the creature. His entire perception shifted when he heard, above a quiet rush of the wind through the plants, a strangely familiar voice, deep and melodious. "And how long are you going to lie there wondering about it with your nose plowed into the dirt and grass?"

Anybody lifted his head hopefully. There he saw a man dressed all in flowing purple robes with white hair avalanching across his shoulders. The man's eyes were deep and Anybody couldn't decide what color they really were.

"Where am I?" he asked, pulling himself to a sitting position.

"Here."

"But where, where? This could be the middle of nowhere."

"No, no, no," chuckled the man, his white hair moving fluidly. "This could be the edge of nowhere, but it certainly isn't the middle." This seemed to delight him and he sat there on his rock, his white hair shaking, laughing quietly to himself while Anybody looked on.

Anybody wanted to question him further but he thought that would be useless. So, glancing back over his shoulder, he began to move along the edge of the woods to the right. After he had traveled some distance, he became aware of a shadow that seemed always to move just inside the line of woods about 100 meters behind him. His body felt particularly alert; the quiet was unnerving. Each time he glanced directly at the spot where he thought the shadow was, there was nothing there. The wood line, although far from regular, seemed to turn gradually to the left.

It was late in the afternoon when Anybody came across a path leading into the woods. He hesitated and then decided to try the path, reasoning that it must lead to where some people were. He had hardly gone more than 100 meters into the woods when there was a rush and sound of movement behind him. Looking back, he saw a shimmering, constantly changing shape that blotted out the light coming down the path.

It was wholly outside of his experience and he was frightened. As the figure advanced up the path toward him, he carefully tried to calm himself, saying over and over again, "There's no reason to be afraid. No reason to be afraid." The more he said it the more afraid he felt.

Suddenly the unknown creature rushed toward him with a cry. Anybody no longer had control over his body. His thoughts vanished and he came to his senses. With a single smooth motion, he turned and raced down the path. He felt very light as he sped on; although he was frightened out of his wits, he heard himself giggle.

The sound of the unknown creature came closer and he thought he felt its warm breath on his head. Just then he caught sight of a bridge across a rushing stream and a house on the other side. Urging himself to expend all his energy, he flashed across the bridge to the house. Without hesitation, or wondering whether anybody was home, he leaped to the door, opened it and rushed in, slamming the door behind him as he did. He heard the thump of a heavy body hitting the door above the sound of thousands and thousands of tiny bells as he collapsed into a heap on the floor.

"And who are you now?" boomed a low, melodious voice that quickly deteriorated into thunderous laughter. Then he caught the first waft of sweet, cool morning air. He ever so slowly opened his eyes. The sound of rushing water came from behind him and as he carefully rolled over, he caught sight of the tumbling, sparkling water that streamed by him only a few meters away. His eyes darted all around and then returned to their original resting point.

As he struggled to stand, Anybody became aware of wholly new and foreign sensations. This gave him pause. He tore his eyes away from his surroundings, glancing for the first time down at his hands-paws-hands-paws. He heard a strangled cry and only later realized that it had come from his own throat. His hands or paws or whatever they were shimmered in the light that flickered through the leaves of the trees above him. His hands were somehow insubstantial. At times he seemed to be able to see through them—they felt incredibly flexible and yet strong. His entire body was covered with the same shimmering, fur-like substance. He found that he was equally comfortable on two and on four legs. A portion of his mind was frozen in terror and amazement and refused to accept what he was seeing and feeling. He noticed that he was able to hear with more acuteness than he had ever experienced—as the wind moved gently through the leaves above, he could detect the sounds given off by each branch of leaves. They were as different from one another as different people's voices. The shifting wind created an extemporaneous concert throughout the trees above and around. He allowed his eyes to close and he became immersed in a sea of sound.

As he listened, Anybody felt different parts of his body resounding to the changes in the strength and tones of the wind-leaves. He opened his eyes and was startled to see that his body glowed and flashed in rapidly changing patterns of colors, completely attuned to the enveloping concert of sound. How long Anybody stood thus entranced he never knew.

Suddenly through the flowing, soothing movement of sounds came a demand for attention. It was partly a smell, partly a taste; he felt the hair of his back stiffen and rise as his body lengthened and flattened itself. An almost inaudible low growl escaped from his clenched teeth. Without any conscious decision on his part, his body whirled, orienting itself away from the passing stream and out towards an area where the woods seemed less thick.

The sun was almost directly overhead as he waited in the shadows of the woods, rapidly scanning the fields that lay before him. Directly ahead at some distance he could see someone striding rapidly toward the woods. As soon as he detected the approaching figure, he froze in position; his eyes fastened unwaveringly on it and he felt his ears rotate forward. The sounds of the man's breathing, his footfalls and of his light green clothing brushing against the grass and bushes came distinctly to him.

As the man approached the woods, Anybody could hear a sudden change in his breathing and he saw a rigidity in the man's movements.

Alarmed by these changes, Anybody lowered himself still closer to the ground. Abruptly the man appeared to shoot forward off the path and fall out of Anybody's sight behind a large rock in the tall grasses. The top of the rock was enveloped in a strange shimmer and Anybody thought that he caught sight of traces of purple and red there. Without warning, his body turned smoothly and loped back into the woods toward the stream that he had awoken besides. He tried to regain some control over his body but it wasn't until his nose and mouth were completely covered by the rushing water in the stream that he had any.

The part of his mind that had at first refused to accept what his senses had told him about the body he found himself in demanded that he exercise his control and return to the edge of the woods to determine what had become of the man he had seen and heard there. Something in Anybody's body resisted, and after what seemed like an interminable struggle, he began to move slowly towards the edge of the woods.

When he reached the place where he had watched from before, he was unable to detect the strange shimmering above the rock. In fact even the rock was gone. This gave him pause. Then, with another involuntary jerk of his head, he noticed the movement of a light green figure far to his left.

He spent much of the afternoon trailing the figure dressed in green. He could approach only to a certain distance before his body would refuse to move closer. Somehow he knew that it was important for him to make contact with the man. He allowed his body to keep track of the man while he plotted furiously, trying to find a way of tricking his body into approaching closer to the man.

Then he stumbled upon a plan. Regaining his balance, he began to suggest softly with words and pictures of food. He worked desperately to find a way to tap directly into the creature's experience of eating. After a short pause there was a surge of energy, and he felt the saliva dripping from his mouth and his hands–paws–hands–paws clenched and unclenched involuntarily, the claws extending and retracting.

He continued this as he forced his eyes to remain fastened on the man in light green moving along the edge of the woods only 100 meters away. His body responded immediately and went into a low crouch, moving swiftly and silently toward the man. When he had halved the distance between himself and the man, he projected messages of danger and fear. The man's body immediately responded by freezing. He giggled and congratulated himself.

By alternately projecting different memories he had learned to tap in the unknown creature's body, he was able to control its movements very well. Periodically, a new smell or sound, or the flicker of a movement in the woods, would override the control he had achieved, but he learned to re-gain control.

The man in light green turned into the woods along one of the paths. Any-body listened and watched carefully, knowing that he would soon have his chance. Allowing the man to enter some distance along the path into the woods, Anybody rushed to the point where the path entered the woods. He had moved openly and the man turned toward him and stopped.

Anybody was willing to wait at first, but then the thought came to him that perhaps the man also wished to make contact. This excited him and with a cry he rushed forward toward the man, who turned abruptly away and began to run down the path further into the woods.

He quickly fed his body the food suggestions and bounded up the path after the man. It took all of his new skill to control his body and prevent it from leaping on to the back of the fleeing man. The creature's body was so engrossed in the chase, each muscle in his legs stretching for speed, that it failed to notice they were approaching a bridge and a cottage on the other side of the stream.

At this point Anybody was making leaps and bounds that covered 15–20 feet at a time. It was in mid-bound that he became aware that the man was gone and had been replaced by a door. This information did him no good as he slammed into the door with a resounding thud. He fell to the ground in front of the door, unaware of the tinkling of thousands and thousands of tiny bells.

Time seemed suspended. All he knew was wet and fast. He dimly and indistinctly recalled something of a low, melodious voice, a glittering ball of mist, and something else . . .

And then, slowly, so slowly, deeply rooted, pushed gently by the passing wind and washed by the rain, he swayed slowly, so slowly. He heard only the dimmest and most indistinct suggestions of a glowing ball of crystal and a voice that demanded his attention. And others, too far from words to recall now. Then he heard another voice.

"And who are you now?" insisted the low, deep voice.

He was again on/in the chair-couch, watching the mists swirl through the interior of the ball of crystal. "I'm still Anybody."

"And do you now know how you know you are Anybody?"

"No."

"Do you understand better how to really be Anybody?"

He hesitated and sank into a reverie. After a long silence the voice said, "Alright, goodbye for now."

He felt a strange foreboding and as he caught the first waft of sweet, cool, morning air, he forced himself to his feet and yelled, "Stop."

"Yes?"

"This can't go on, this can't go on."

"Really, what do you think will stop it?" inquired the voice with a suggestion of humor.

"Every time I wake up, it's morning and I smell the sweet, cool morning air . . . and . . . I . . ." He was at a loss for words.

"Would you rather wake up in the hot, sticky afternoon, or perhaps at night?" intoned the voice with concern.

"No, no, that's not it. I'm doing the same things over and over again."

"Yes, I've noticed. You must be rather good at them now, mustn't you?"

"Yes, . . . no . . . I mean, yes . . ."

"Extraordinary," commented the voice unhelpfully. "What is it exactly you want?"

"You haven't answered my question—who are you?" he said, surprising himself with that information.

"Well, well," said the voice, chuckling softly. "I am a nervomism."

"What?" he demanded.

"A nervomism—and I must really warn you that I can answer only three of your questions, and I've already answered two."

"That's not true—what was the second question I asked?" he demanded with some force.

"You asked first who I was, and then when I answered, you asked, 'What?' and so I repeated that answer—that's two. Now if you think that's silly, consider the fact that this is the answer to your third question— you've used up all of your questions," the voice replied sternly, "and that's dumb."

"Please, please, can you give me one more question?" he cried desperately.

"Well, at least be clever enough to ask me for two so that when I answer your question, you will have one left to use," instructed the voice.

"Yes, yes, can you give me two more, please?"

"All right, ask away but make it interesting."

"Who decides what happens next?" he said, surprising himself.

Anybody was nearly swept away by the thunderous applause that came from every part of the cottage. As the applause died, he heard the deep, rich laughter of the voice, and then, "What specifically do you want to know about what happens next?"

"I've been a man dressed in green and I know two routes to get from the tree to here. I've been other things too, things that I don't understand or at least I don't think I have words for right now. But what I really want to know is: who decides what I will be the next time around?" He paused, out of breath. The room suddenly grew brighter and the sound of the bells came to him. His vision blurred and when his eyes refocused, he discovered that he was sitting between two people. On one side was a man with long, fine, white hair and flowing purple robes. On the other was a woman dressed entirely in red with black hair spilling over her shoulders and streaming down her back.

Both of them were staring at him as if waiting for him to speak. He wondered what they expected him to say; then they looked at each other and smiled faintly.

He had no idea how long they smiled at each other; time stood still. "What does it mean for time to stand still?" asked the man, peering intently out from under his bushy eyebrows at Anybody.

"Act as if everything were normal," advised the woman in a low, urgent voice. His entire body jerked when he heard her voice and he felt alarmed by the implication of what she had said.

"Can you answer this question?" said the man, with his faint smile returning.

"Obey this command," whispered the woman, suppressing a laugh.

As his eyes closed he felt each of them take hold of his arms. He wanted to protest but he was caught up in the sensations of movement as they maneuvered his arms, holding them at the wrist and elbow. At first they seemed to move together and apart and then together again.

He was flooded with images and voices that seemed to come from within. He lost track of the movements of his body. He felt the fresh wind ruffle his hair. The sounds around him were soft and muted. There was music coming from his left, a great distance away.

He slowly opened his eyes. With the first images, he screamed and closed them. He slowly became aware of a soothing voice murmuring in his ear that he was safe and to not be afraid of what he saw.

The voice coaxed him to try again. He again opened his eyes and after a few seconds he was able to calm himself, regulating his breathing until he could relax.

He was standing on the edge of a tremendous cliff. Before him stretched land, woods, mountains, ocean. Wherever he turned his eyes and ears, he could see and hear what was occurring there. The sudden changes in what he saw and heard unnerved him and he was reluctant to move lest he lose control again. His eyes and ears felt drawn to a wooded area far below and away to his left. He turned his full attention there.

He presently focused on a small cottage. The roof seemed to dissolve before his very eyes and he beheld a young man dressed in green, refreshing himself at a table. He then heard his voice roll firmly across the intervening space, filling the cottage. The young man moved to a space directly in front of a faintly glowing ball of crystal.

"Settle yourself all the way down," he gently instructed the young man. "I am ready to answer your questions—ask them," he said. As he did, he heard the faint and not unpleasant sound of the laughter of a man and a woman. Glancing up, he caught a glimpse of streaks of purple and red soaring off into the sky. He turned back just in time to hear the young man dressed in green ask, "Who are you?"

Anybody began to dream, though he could not quite remember all the details. He saw a Princess riding upon a horse, a sad King and a large fire. He saw a mysterious object of crystal that shined and glistened and he became both intrigued and afraid. Finally he saw himself walking down a long tunnel and entering a forest. He moved slowly through the forest into a clearing and there sat an old man with white hair and bright purple robes. The old man turned to Anybody and, as if he had been expecting him all along, he said, "What do you want?"

Anybody heard himself say, "I want to be somebody, somebody special."

The old man laughed and said, "You poor fool, you have been somebody special all along but you just don't know it." The old man in purple began to laugh to himself, he roared and roared until Anybody couldn't stand the sound of his laughter. So he ran at the old man but as he did, he found himself running on a cloud and the more he tried to run, the more his body stayed in one place. As he stopped running his body would fall.

"I'm trapped, I'm trapped," he yelled. Kicking and yelling, he awoke from his dream only to find there were no scholars and no Blink. In fact, there was no forest, no clearing, no tree, just Anybody, who felt somewhat better off for at least knowing who he was.

 nybody and Time

Anybody was slowly coming to his senses and recalling what a good meal he had when he last ate. Suddenly he was aware that he was not in a bed or in a dream but that his back was lying on the hard ground. He thought to himself, "Not again, surely, all this must end somewhere." He began to open his eyes and he said to himself, "Wait, it might be better to just go into a dream."

But as his head cleared bit by bit, he finally agreed with himself that this might be a dream and in fact might even be a nice place. However, his eyes slowly opened, the bright sun blurred his vision, and all he could see were wavy lines. He felt nauseous for a moment, and then looked very hard, blinking over and over, shaking his head back and forth.

The world finally held still. He found himself sitting up on a cliff overlooking a beautiful valley. He said out loud, but really to himself, "How did I get here? And where is here, I wonder?"

To his surprise a voice answered, "Here is here of course, where else could here be?"

Anybody swirled around as fast as he could, and there looking down on him was emptiness. He had so expected to see someone that Anyone was spellbound. Not knowing how to see no one there, he finally sighed and, slapping himself across the face, he said, "Now I'm really in trouble. I'm hearing voices and there is nobody there. I must be losing my mind."

The voice, however, replied (much to Anybody's surprise), "So I'm nobody, am I?"

Anybody whirled around again and looked all over but still he could see no one. Somehow in his confusion he did manage to apologize. "I am very sorry but . . . I mean . . . I am sorry, but you surprised me and I can't seem to see you."

"That's right!" the voice answered. "And like most fools, just because you can't see something you assume that it isn't there, don't you?"

Now, not just Anybody believed that seeing was believing; many other well-respected people believed this. And, as Anybody told the voice, it seemed to be a rational way of behaving. The voice scoffed at Anybody, who was being logical. "Hachhh fool, silly fool, have you ever had a cold?"

"Why yes, I have," replied Anybody.

"Did you believe it was there?"

"Why, of course it was there!"

"Could you see it?" exclaimed the voice.

Anybody became confused and protested it was not the same thing. The voice went on and on making its point. "How about air? Do you believe in air, or love? How about friendship?" Finally Anybody, who by now was forced to give in, asked the voice what it was like to live without any body.

The voice broke into laughter. It roared and roared and finally asked, "What makes you think I don't have any body, just because you can't see it?"

"Well, I just assumed."

"You assumed," the voice came back harshly. "You assumed too much. That's the nature of your problem, you know. Don't you?"

Anybody assured the voice that he didn't know. In fact, he didn't know anything except that he was Anybody. He told the voice, "I don't know where I am or even what time it is."

The voice roared with laughter and said, as if imitating the voice of an older man, "Time eahhh what does time mean? Time doesn't mean anything at all." It continued to laugh. "What does it mean to have a book read? It doesn't mean anything at all, does it?"

Anybody could only reply that as far as he could tell nothing didn't mean anything at all. But as he said it, he was sure it sounded stupid. The voice, however, said, "Hey, that's catchy, nothing doesn't mean anything at all." With that the voice said, "You know, we're gonna get along just fine."

And then a bright light blinded Anybody, who happened to be looking, and pooooofffff, there before him stood the figure of a man. "Where did you come from?" shouted Anybody, who was startled. You see, he was quite confused about all this.

The figure stepped up, laughing, and said, "Do not concern yourself from whence I came; it is enough that I am here and that you can see me. If you really knew how to know, you would have known I was here all along and then you would have seen me. But we do not have time for this. We must be off. Are you ready?"

"For what?" Anybody protested.

"To meet her, of course," the figure replied in an astonished tone. "Don't you know?"

"Know what?" Anybody insisted.

The figure roared with laughter, which, by the way, made Anybody very nervous because he did not know what the man was laughing at, so, of course, he assumed he must be laughing at him, and he did not like being laughed at. And so he stood patiently by, while the man laughed and looked like he was not in the least concerned.

At last the man stopped laughing and said to Anybody, who was listening quite attentively, "Let us be off. All this is very silly and there is really something much more important at hand."

Anybody instinctively jumped up and followed the stranger, but all at once he stopped and demanded, "Why should I go with you? Who are you? What is so important?"

The stranger turned around slowly and peered at Anybody and then slowly began to speak. "It is not for you to question why. As for who I am, you might say I'm one who serves people like you who are lost in a very special sense of the word lost, but that, of course, would only be one way of describing who I am."

Anybody protested, "You must have a name. . ."

"A name, what is in a name?"

Anybody was ready for any further nonsense and replied, "There are letters in a name, or if it is not written then at least there are sounds."

"So there are," the stranger conceded, "and in my name there are four letters: T-I-M-E."

Anybody recognized at once that this spelled "time," but he thought that time was a queer thing for someone to be named. But when your name is Anybody, you really can't mention such a thought. So he was content with that and he pressed on for more relevant information. "Where are we going, Time?"

"To her," he answered.

Suddenly Anybody remembered what Time had said just a few minutes ago: "What does Time mean? It doesn't mean anything at all." Anybody interrupted even though it was a change of subject. "Time does too mean something. It means you."

Time ignored this and continued on his way, stating that Anybody firmly understood she shouldn't be kept waiting. With this, Time ran on and Anybody followed as best he could, figuring it is better to be somewhere with Time than somewhere without.

They ran for about an hour when they reached a large mountain that loomed up out of nowhere. Anybody stopped and looked up at the mountain, which was very high and very solemn standing there all alone. He turned to Time and said, "I'm too tired and I'm hungry. I won't climb up there unless you give me a good reason." Time, who by now was just

about out of patience with Anybody, stated that both food and rest were at the top and that only rest was here at the bottom. Before Anybody could say anything Time was on his way up and Anybody plodded behind.

It seemed like hours before they reached the top, but finally both Anybody and Time were standing at the edge of a magnificent garden. Anybody could see no house or castle, nothing but garden. He looked all

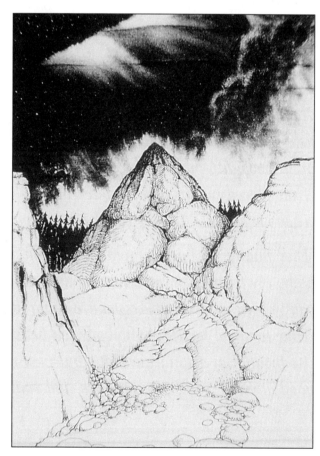

around, wondering what was up here that was so important. Time, who must have been reading Anybody's thoughts, assured him that there was no house but that there was plenty of food. "You understand," Time went on, "the lady has great power and so it never rains all over the garden at once or gets too hot. There is no need to hide from nature. Nature and the lady are good friends and they both have used their great powers to build this garden."

By this point Anybody had really taken kind of a liking to Time, though he did wish he would change his name. They walked into the garden and Anybody admired its beauty. Presently they came to a clearing, a green field in the center of which was a stone pavilion with a waterfall filling a great pool. An oaken table laden with a great feast stood by the pool. Time placed his arm on the back of Anybody and led him to the table. They ate and ate till they could eat no more.

They finally sat back, sipping wine, and Time began to speak. "Anybody, my friend, you may not know much about who you are, or where you've been, or even where you are going, but you sure know how to eat." Time laughed heartily. Anybody felt better than he had in a long time. He thought of asking questions but then decided it never does him any good anyway, so he just sat back and smiled.

Presently Anybody fell asleep, and though he could not quite remember his dreams, he saw a tremendous fountain that sprayed the most wondrous water. He felt himself lifted into the air and floating through space. He saw the sorcerer in the purple robes and heard him whisper in his ear, but he could not understand.

Then suddenly he became aware that he was sleeping and (even worse) that he was waking up. His mind raced, his heart pounded; he thought, "Where will I be now? And just when I had found a place I liked." Slowly he opened his eyes and sighed with relief. He was still in the garden. And Time was still with him, sitting by the pond swishing his feet in the water and poking his fingers between the stones of the pavilion. He noticed Anybody was watching and turned to him. "So, you awaken, my sleepy head. Too much wine I dare say, but the lady decided to let you sleep, so sleep you had and you had better wash yourself and be presentable to meet her."

Anybody washed and followed Time through the forest to another clearing. Then he saw her and stopped cold in his tracks.

She was not soft and gentle as he had expected, the delicate fantasy of a kind, helpful lady. She was tall and fierce, yet in her own way she was more beautiful than any woman he had ever seen. She wore robes of bright red, and she was like a huge crimson rose in the middle of the green garden. She did not turn or make any sign of being aware of the approaching two, yet Anybody could sense that

she knew they were there. She spoke at last, slowly, and Anybody detected a clever tone behind well-chosen words.

"You are here at last. I had dreamed you would come. Was the journey difficult?" She turned and gazed at Anybody, who was watching her.

"What do you want from me?" Anybody inquired in the most casual voice he could muster; underneath he was terrified.

"A favor," she replied. She seemed to be searching for something, eyeing Anybody as closely as she could. Anybody was surprised but still scared.

"What could such a great person like you want from me? Why, I don't even know. . ." His voice trailed off because the lady was shaking her head "no," and he did not know what she was signaling "no" to. So he went silent. She smiled at him and he felt different, more at ease.

She said, "Do not be afraid. I will not hurt you, and the favor I need I will explain later. For now just be my welcomed guest."

Anybody spent the next three days in the garden. He spent time with the Lady and with Time, though he could find out almost nothing. They would just laugh and give him silly answers. He asked the Lady her name but she said, "I might be called a sorceress or a witch, or I might be called a princess, but never will I tell my name to Anybody, for in my name lies great power."

At the end of the third day Time came and got Anybody from the pool where he was bathing. They went back to the second clearing. The Lady sat on a velvet couch, and as Anybody entered the clearing, marveling at her beauty, he gasped. To the Lady's right was the Sorcerer in purple.

Anybody fell to his knees and begged for mercy. The Sorcerer jumped up in anger. "Stop this, pull yourself together, we have no time for your sniveling." Anybody, stopping with a jolt, stood up and faced the two powerful figures. The old Sorcerer sat down. "That's better, my boy. You get a hold of yourself. You have to face much worse than me before this is through."

Anybody was struck with fear. "Before what is through?" he trembled.

The Sorcerer motioned with his hand for Anybody to sit down. "Now, listen carefully, my boy, you have much to learn and much to do. You must forgive us for the way you arrived, but we had to be very sure that no one knew who you were."

"Well, you shouldn't have any problem there," Anybody retorted. "I don't even know who I am."

"Believe me," the Sorcerer cautioned him, "it is just as well you don't know who you are really." Anybody was very concerned at all this and his worry showed all over his face.

The Lady looked at him softly and reassured him that as long as he didn't know who he really was, no one could have power over him or power to hurt him. She went on to tell him, "The power to cast spells lies in knowing which words to use with each specific person. Their name is the most powerful, along with words from their history. We all have histories, though we have kept them very secret, and we have kept our names very secret as well. The evil powers with which we have to contend know much about us. They have many spies, and our powers up until now have been evenly matched with theirs.

"But recently all of us here have received a deadly blow. We, the wise ones, who have for centuries protected all the worlds to our rear, are now in jeopardy. The master of the unknown has learned my name and perhaps the names of my noble friends who reside here with me. We can feel that our powers are waning, and the fate of those who are protected by us unknowingly is at stake.

"We have selected you from among them to aid us in our hour of need. You are shielded by your own ignorance and we wish for you to go forth as our army."

Anybody could not believe his ears. He was both honored and terrified. He looked back at the Lady in astonishment. "But how can I be an army?"

The Sorcerer interrupted. "Yes, exactly what does it mean for one man to be an army? This is your task. You must go forth into the domain of the Unknown; you alone must cross the barrier where none of us have dared to tread. But more important, you must return and bring with you information, vital information about the master of the Unknown reaches of the beyond. Do you now understand?" The Sorcerer eyed Anybody, who was watching him and listening to him.

Anybody screamed, "I can't . . . don't make me do it, I am . . . I mean . . . I . . ." He began to sob and whimper.

The Sorcerer slapped him and shook him. "Get a hold of yourself. You are but one small particle in a huge universe. Have you really so much to lose?"

Anybody suddenly came to his senses. What the Sorcerer had said crystalized in his mind. He really had nothing, so he had nothing to lose. He thought to himself, "I will risk all the nothing I have and face the Unknown in search of something." This gave him a sense of purpose – this was something worth having nothing for.

He turned from fear to stone-cold resolution. He took a deep breath and turned to the Lady, who had been patiently watching his outburst. "I will go, I will do what you ask. Facing the Unknown out there could be no worse than facing all that I don't know here."

The Lady and the Sorcerer smiled and they all ate a great feast together. The wise ones were called together. They instructed Anybody in what they knew of the method of their adversary. He was instructed in spells and counterspells, word magic and thing magic, hexes and counterhexes – all the knowledge they believed might be an asset to their brave warrior.

Anybody slept well that night and practiced his new skills all the next week. Finally the Sorcerer came to him and said, "My friend, you must be off. Time will be your guide as far as he can, then you will be on your own. Practice you might need, but it would only be dangerous history that could be used against you. Be off now. I wish you a safe and speedy return, but do not return without some of his history or there will most likely be nowhere to return to."

The Sorcerer patted Anybody on the back and led him to the edge of the mountain. Time had compiled provisions for both of them; these they took upon their backs and began their journey.

Anybody and Time came down the mountain and passed quickly and quietly for two days through thick forest until they reached a clearing. Anybody could see for miles and miles. There was only nothing and more nothing. A great plain lay before them. Time turned back to Anybody and extended his hand in friendship. Somehow Anybody could tell they were about to part.

Time said, "This is it, my fearless companion. We must part, for I can go no further." Anybody wished that his companion would continue on the journey, but he knew it would be fruitless to ask him to continue.

So Anybody said goodbye and went on alone. Time stood still and watched him walk on. Anybody turned around just in time to see Time dissolve in thin air—poooofffff. And now Anybody knew that he was surely on his own.

The days passed slowly. Anybody crossed the great plain and came to a forest. It was unlike any forest he had ever seen, and with some reservation he entered and made his way into the trees. As he passed slowly through miles of trees, he watched and listened but nothing out of the ordinary could be perceived. Yet he knew that more than the odd trees around him accounted for his feeling of uneasiness.

Something suddenly struck him from behind. He turned around so quickly that he saw the pebble that had struck him falling to the ground. He was so terrified that everything appeared to be in slow motion. He lifted his gaze and was face-to-face with a queer old man, bent and stooped by the years, dressed as a pauper.

"Have you any food to share with an old man who is hungry?"

Anybody was so relieved that he pulled some bread from his pack and handed it to the old man. The old man began to eat and peered at Anybody out of the corners of his eyes. "Who are you, my dear young man who comes walking in my forest alone and unprotected from the forces that lie here within?"

Anybody, who had relaxed somewhat, became tense again. "I . . . I am just Anybody and I am going . . ." He became aware that he had no destination. "I have no . . . I . . . ker a . . . aa."

The old man interrupted. "Are you running away from someone?"

"Yes, yes I am and I don't know where I am going."

The old man seemed pleased at all this. "And you don't know where you are going?"

Anybody tried to grasp the moment. "I have no future as of now and I am looking for one." He stated this with as much conviction as he could.

The old man began to speak in riddles, which Anybody could not understand. The old man rattled on and on. "Running horse, slithering snake, laughing spell, disappearing act . . ."

Suddenly it occurred to Anybody that the old man was trying to attack him with magic. "What are you doing?" Anybody demanded of the old man.

"Nothing," the old man conceded. "I was just talking to myself, but who are you really that trespasses in my woods?"

Anybody assured the old man that he would be glad to leave if the old man would show him the way. But the old man shook his head "no" and drew a huge sword from under his cloak. The old man no longer looked old but rather like a great warrior cast in bronze, fearless and deadly.

Anybody was filled with fright. His mind raced through all the Sorcerer had told him until a description of this guardian of the forest passed through his mind. He called out, "You may find it so handy that it will give you a lift!" He glanced at the arm and hand that held the sword. It began to rise up.

"I can handle that," said the old man-turned-warrior, and his movement stopped. He smiled at Anybody and said, "Yes I can, but only as quickly as your heart attacks."

"Naturally," intoned Anybody, "as soon as you can respond fully to my riddle."

"Pray, begin to continue," said the old man/warrior.

Anybody began: "Head is to hat as body is to ————, and I am to my as you are to ————, and crosses are to 'T's as dots are to '————s' comfortably."

And even as the old man/warrior's eyelids grew heavy, Anybody heard him whisper, "You must be frozen with anticipation."

Anybody felt paralyzed and a cold chill ran up his spine. The old man/warrior began to move forward blindly, his sword still suspended. "You will come up against no stumbling block if only you always put your best foot forward," said Anybody haltingly.

The old man/warrior slowed and he continued to inch his right leg toward Anybody while his left was left.

Anybody chuckled and said, "Amazing—you give them an inch and they take a mile—that could give you a splitting headache." Anybody could tell that the guardian of the forest was beginning to crack up. "Pull your-self together!!" commanded Anybody cuttingly. "Remember it could have been worse—you might have been a chip off the old block or a spitting image or my cup of tea or a bag of hot wind."

"Enough," cried the guardian, who looked quite withered by the experience.

"Not quite. I think that you're due to sit for a spell," said Anybody, casting about for an appropriate next move.

"I'd rather lie," replied the guardian truthfully.

"Of course," said Anybody acidly, "but it might burn you up."

The guardian screamed but Anybody caused him to flush and wash away the irritating sensations. "Sleep deeply, O Guardian, with a song in your heart and a pocket full of dreams, until I call for you," directed Anybody, and he went on his way.

He was very tired and very afraid yet quite impressed with his new powers. He had learned better than he had suspected from the teachings he had received, but now he only desired to rest for a short time. He found a place with shelter and settled down to sleep.

The sword fell to the ground and the figure turned old and withered again. "Do not destroy me," he begged. "I did not know you were one of power."

Anybody placed the guardian into a deep sleep and went on his way.

Immediately Anybody entered a dream, or what he thought was a dream. He felt his mind struggling to open many doors that had been very tightly shut; one by one they would open and there would be nothing inside. Time and time again he struggled to open a door, just to find an empty room.

He then became aware that it was not his mind at all that was searching—it was his mind that was being searched. He struggled to awaken but he could not. He fought with himself to achieve consciousness and finally did, but he was no longer in the forest or still asleep. He was standing in a courtyard devoid of people except for one whom he could not see. This one spoke from within a tent of silken veils situated in the center of the courtyard. "Why are you here?"

"I don't really know!" Anybody answered.

"Do you come to match your powers against mine?" The voice was hard and unyielding.

"Oh, no, I am kind of lost," Anybody assured the voice.

"They have sent you from the mountain. In their folly they underestimated me once again and you have walked into your death." A figure emerged through the veils. Anybody watched both intrigued and horrified at how much this person

knew and the mention of his death. But he had volunteered to die and if he had to he would.

A huge figure stepped out from the tent. It had the body of a man with the head of a bear, or so it appeared. He had no normal hands but giant claws with long talons. Anybody stepped back and gasped with horror. "How could I hurt you? I am so small and you are fierce."

The figure stopped and peered at Anybody. "You know how, don't you?"

Anybody protested that he was just dreaming; none of this was real, and no one can hurt anyone else in a dream. Pooooffffff. The figure was no longer a monster but only a man like any other.

"What have you done?" the figure demanded.

"I have done nothing," Anybody protested.

"So we are to match power against power, are we?"

"No," Anybody protested. He decided it was time to be very careful. "I have just come to meet with one so powerful that we might become allies. If I am welcome let us talk as friends do."

The man eyed him carefully and thoughtfully and then clapped his hands and yelled, "Table, food, wine, music for my guest." Suddenly a table laden with a great feast appeared, and behind it musicians already playing. Finally the man extended his hand to Anybody and said, "You may call me the one who guides. How may I be of service to you?"

Anybody was at a loss to answer. "I am Anybody; I seek to understand."

"To understand what?" The man peered at him.

"The ways of the unknown." And before Anybody could say another word, the man said, "So be it," and clapped his hands.

Anybody found himself lying on a hillside overlooking a great city. He thought at first he must have awakened from his dream, but to his dismay he still held his wine glass in his hand.

Anybody walked slowly down the hill into a city bustling with people of many strange races. Everyone in the city seemed to have a purpose and to be in a hurry. Anybody just strolled along, wondering what would happen next.

A soldier approached him and looked him squarely in the eye. "Follow me," he said. "Follow me."

Anybody followed the soldier to a great palace and was taken to the quarters of the soldiers. The captain of the guards was a giant man who carried a tremendous staff. He was scolding the younger soldiers for brawling when Anybody approached him. The soldier who had escorted Anybody presented him by name (so to speak); this surprised Anybody, as he had never met any of these people before.

The captain turned to Anybody and looked him over. "So you wish to be a soldier."

"It was not my intention, no," answered Anybody.

"He sent you, didn't he?" the Captain persisted.

"I guess he did," Anybody replied.

"Well, let's begin now." The captain signaled for Anybody to follow him and led him to a courtyard where soldiers were practicing with swords and staffs. They were all large men and quick of hand. The sound of clashing steel rung in Anybody's ears and he wondered if he could even stand the piercing sound. The old man handed Anybody a large sword; he could barely hold it.

The Captain demanded, "Strike me." Anybody thought that attacking the Captain was a preposterous idea.

He retorted, "I will not."

The Captain swung his huge staff and a blow fell on Anybody's chest. He fell down, gulping for air, and rose with fire in his eyes. He was furious. Something in him clicked. His mind raced through discussions of the armies of the Unknown and he cried out in anger, "STOP, STOP, I SAY, DOWN on your knees!"

The courtyard became silent—swords and spears fell like rain. A hundred men fell to their knees and the captain was thrown over backwards. Anybody held out his hand in a gesture of strength and all obeyed him. They begged for mercy before him. He turned and left the courtyard.

He entered the palace, feeling invincible. A mere gesture from his hand and the guards would fall to their knees. He walked straight into the throne room and the attendants parted before him. As they did, he saw the one who guides on his throne smiling.

"A brilliant performance, my friend." He began to clap.

But Anybody was not amused. He peered at the figure on the throne and reached from within his mind to the mind of the one who guides. They struggled; time stood still. The tension built to a climax. The one who guides fell to his knees and crawled before his new master.

The one who guides rose to his feet as his face filled with hatred. He looked down at Anybody, who was watching him, and said, "Do not overestimate yourself, little one. I am not a mere Captain."

Anybody could feel the great power of the one who guides blocking his thoughts from entering. The one who guides smiled queerly. "Do you wish a journey? Go into your thoughts—you can GO NOW!"

Anybody's mind went blank for a second. As his thoughts began to race he heard in the back of his mind, "Do not let him distract you." He regained his train of thought and let a burst of anger from his hand. But to his amazement he was standing in front of a great mirror. Or was it a mirror? There were two of him; he decided it must be the guide.

They moved in unison. Anybody was unsure who was leading and who was following. Anybody became somewhat unnerved by this but he remained steadfast and poured his thoughts upon the one who guides. The self-image of Anybody turned into the one who guides, but still they moved in circles, as cats before the battle, matching both strength of will and body.

The one who guides broke the silence with a burst of spells. "Isn't Anybody going blank a little bit? What do I mean by what I say? Isn't Anybody falling down and down?" Anybody blocked out the spells by looking quickly at the one who guides' foot as if something were happening to it. The guide instinctively glanced down at his foot and Anybody yelled, "Silence." Again the two stared at each other will-to-will, eye-to-eye in a battle of power.

Anybody was draining himself. He could feel his power beginning to wane. He knew he could not keep this up much longer.

Suddenly it occurred to Anybody that perhaps the same thing was happening to the one who guides. He said, "You can FEEL your power waning, you're growing weaker and weaker, now you can feel it draining, waning, draining weaker and meeker NOW!!!"

The one who guides began to look pale. He struggled to regain his strength but Anybody grasped a hold of the moment and threw it at him, knocking the one who guide off balance. They began to cast spells at each other, ducking and dogging, till finally a thought began to crystalize in Anybody's mind.

All the history of the one who guides he had learned from the Sorcerer, all he had seen and heard since his arrival, all he knew of the one who guides in his mind. He gazed at the guide knowingly. The guide fell under the weight of such thoughts, screaming and squirming on the floor. The battle was over.

"Where is he?" Anybody demanded.

"I can't tell you." The guide pleaded with Anybody. But Anybody bent his will until the guide agreed to take him wherever he wished to go.

They set out in the morning, just the two of them. The guide said they were going to a city named Ish where the master resided. They went through many strange places for three days until they were standing at the edge of a pasture, a mile or two on the other side of which stood a city such as Anybody had never seen. Great towers rose up into the sky almost out of sight and glistened with stone, clear and brilliant.

The guide begged, "He will kill me—let me go back now." Anybody agreed and marched on alone, with determination to face what before he had feared without seeing its glory and power.

He approached the city, but as he neared the front gate he sensed, though he was not sure how, power—power such as he had not ever experienced.

He could not enter. He stepped back. There was no guard at the gate so he tried again but the force was too strong—he could not pass the open gate. He became aware that no voices could be heard from within the city—in fact not even a sound.

He camped by the city and waited but he was not sure what he waited for. The sun sank. He grew sleepy, so he curled up and drifted into a deep sleep.

He dreamed of long and terrible wars that were beyond his comprehension. He saw the crowning of a king. But no faces could he see well enough to recognize. He saw a massive oaken door and sensed something horrible behind it, and he saw a small book with engraved letters he could not read. Then he heard the sound of horses hooves, but almost at the same moment realized they were not in his dream.

He sprang to his feet and turned, and there he saw a beautiful princess on a white horse. Just as he felt the first twinge of enjoyment at so lovely a sight, two large men jumped out from the nearby bushes and grabbed the horse. One tried to grab the lovely young woman.

Anybody cried out instinctively. His scream was shrill and loud. The two men stopped dead in their tracks. They drew swords, but Anybody raised his hand and the swords fell to the ground. His anger swelled up. He was so hot he screamed again and the two men burst into flames and ran off into the woods. The beautiful lady rode back into the city.

Anybody felt proud that he had been so helpful, yet he wished the lady had stopped and spoken with him.

He once again tried to enter the city but could not. He was very frustrated; he sighed and sat back down again. Then he heard a voice calling from within the city walls. "Enter and be welcome. The Master is grateful for your service to him. He wishes to reward such valor."

Anybody entered the city; this time he felt no force repelling him. He was greeted by a page who took him to a guest house. Still he saw or heard no one in the city, just himself and the page. He bathed and was brought new clothes, and was led into a hall with blazing fires at either end. There he waited!

Presently, the princess entered. She was the most beautiful woman he had ever seen, perhaps more beautiful than even the Sorceress. She thanked him and spoke of other things, but he became mesmerized by the tone of her voice. He was lost in her words, swimming like one in the ocean being dunked by waves and coming up for air now and again.

Suddenly she looked over her shoulder and thanked him again and left. The room was silent. The ground began to rumble. Anybody looked up and noticed a great oaken door. Slowly the door opened and he felt a source of immense power. His will was crumbling under the pressure. He forced himself with all his strength to stand erect. Flames filled the room as the door opened and a being ten times Anybody's height entered, filling the room with his presence. The voice echoed, "Who are you?"

Anybody was shocked and terrified. "Nobody . . . I mean . . . Anybody . . . oh my."

The voice came again. "Do not be frightened too much, little one. You saved my niece from ones who would have held her for ransom. I will not hurt you but I will grant you a favor. What would you have from me that you are at the gates of my city?"

Anybody was quite sure this was not the time to ask for a biography, so he told the master, "I have come to see greatness, to behold it so that my life would have meaning even if I should die for it, and this I have done. I have seen your greatness and the beauty of the one I helped. This is reward enough."

The voice rumbled again. "Surely I can grant you something. What would you desire?"

Anybody was somewhat more relaxed so he ventured a request. "I would ask to take a meal with your niece. I have never seen such beauty and the pleasure of her company would be the greatest gift a man could desire."

The voice roared with laughter. "You're a strange one, but I detect there is power in you also. I will grant your wish, and we will meet again if I am not wrong. You have some other purpose, do you not?"

Anybody felt his every thought was being searched. He focused his attention on the princess. The oaken door closed and Anybody collapsed to the floor. He was very strained.

He was taken to his guest house and there he waited till the page returned and led him to a garden where a meal had been laid upon a table. And he ate and talked and laughed with the princess. She was lonely, so she was willing to talk, but knew nothing of her uncle except that after her parents were killed he had cared for her. She saw him rarely and was always afraid when she did. The city had fewer than a hundred people in it—all were servants to the master. The armies were to the west in another city—messengers would come and go, but she knew nothing of what was going on in the world around her. She had wished for years to leave this place but her uncle would not permit it.

Anybody enjoyed his visit and slept well that night in a fine bed. In the morning he had breakfast served to him and then was summoned to the master. He went again to the great hall and there he waited until the master appeared through the oaken door and spoke. "I have decided that whatever mischief you came here to perpetuate, I can make you a better offer. You will stay and be company for my niece. You will be honorable or I shall torture you beyond belief."

The master made an image of dungeons with snakes, and devices of pain came into Anybody's mind. "She is lonely and needs friendship as young women and young men do. Go now, I have other matters to attend to."

Anybody returned to his house and for the next three weeks rode and played and laughed with the princess. It was by far the best time of his life, but always on his mind was the task he had promised to perform. He was free to roam the city, but there was nowhere to go and nothing to discover about the master. He was unsure just what the next move would be.

However, in the course of a conversation that evening, the Princess said she was so surprised when she had found the Master writing in a diary. She told Anybody, who was listening quite attentively now, that the master told her that he keeps a complete record of his whole life so it would be recorded for history's sake.

Anybody thought, "This is my chance to succeed in my endeavor. Possibly I can escape with the diary and the princess." So he set out that night to find the diary.

He walked down the long, narrow street, wondering in which building in which room the diary was kept. His feet moved slowly and carefully along the cobblestone street. He turned around and around wondering, really wondering, in which building the secret was hidden.

Next to the great hall was a massive stone building with long columns down the front and a door eight feet high. Anybody thought to himself, "This might be the place the Master could pass under the door." And perhaps the diary was within. However, Anybody could not open the huge door. In fact, he could not even reach the handle.

So he walked all around until he noticed that he could enter the building by climbing up the side and passing in a window along the top. This took quite some time but he was very determined. When he reached the window he slid inside quite like a cat.

It was very dark, and he could hear a low steady hummmm hummmm hummmm from somewhere in the big building. He slipped down to the floor and began to explore, but he heard faint footsteps—one for each of his. He held his breath, but suddenly he lost his grip and became frightened and slowly turned around, opening his eyes wide as he could.

He was by himself. He did not know what to do; he had never had to face up to himself this way. He had faced up to the guide and the guardian of the forest but now he was beside himself with fright. And he did not know what to do.

Instinctively, he thrust out his arm but he overreached himself. He began to float up as if he were weightless. He looked down at himself for a moment, wondering how he had gotten himself into such a mess.

Anybody was more confused than he had ever been in the whole course of all his doings. At that moment everything in the room began to float—the chairs, the table, everything. Anybody was lost in a swirling conglomeration of objects. Suddenly he looked sideways at himself, but then a wind swept him away down a tunnel. He was ahead of himself and then he surpassed himself and was behind himself.

All this was driving him quite insane when, at that very moment, he must have spread himself too thin because he couldn't figure out which him was the real him. He was all over the place everywhere he looked. And worse yet he was looking from everywhere. No, he had been nowhere and somewhere but he had never been everywhere all at once. So he began to try and pull himself together; one by one he got hold of himself, and he would hold himself back so he didn't go to pieces again.

This whole episode was a shattering one for Anybody. He would grab hold of himself, then he would feel himself slipping away again. Finally, the wind stopped and little by little he collected himself. But he was quite sure that he wasn't all there, so he began to look around. And sure enough, he found himself leaning against the door in a great hall. He gave himself a pat on the back as he asked himself, "How did I go all to pieces so?"

To his surprise he answered himself, "Anybody, just think how many of you there are inside you to become; this is the temple where one learns to find himself." Anybody was quite pleased to discover that talking to himself could be so educational. At last he checked to make sure he was all there and began again to search for the diary. He went back upstairs to the open window and began to climb out and slipped.

Anybody lifted himself off the street. He moved on to the next likely building and went to enter but could not. He tried to pass in the door, but he became frozen with fright, trapped in an impossible actuality. With utter clarity he realized this was more than just a bewildering confrontation. It was a depressing realization. He was not entering a door but falling down, head over heels, twisting and turning down deeper and deeper, falling and falling into what he did not know. Until, splash, he was immersed in very cold water.

He pulled himself out of what appeared to be a large pond. As he crawled up on the rocks he became aware of the sound of laughter. He turned and there were two mysterious men, dressed like wizards, roaring with laughter and slapping each other on the back. Suddenly one of them became very serious and peered at Anybody directly. "Explain yourself," the first wizard demanded. The second wizard laughed even harder.

Anybody replied, "I cannot."

The first wizard continued, "What stops you?" His voice was low and inquiring. Anybody thought this was a most unusual question, but before he could reply the second wizard also became serious and interjected, "Reasons, reasons stop him. Reason stops him from talking and think-ing and smiling and forget-ting and forgiving, and in fact, reason stops him pe-riod." Both wizards again roared with laughter.

Anybody imagined how silly he must have looked falling out of the sky into their pond to two such wise old men. It was really a moving experience. He turned back to apologize, as any polite person would under such circumstances, and to his surprise there was only one wizard and one very large mirror, which seemed to be following Anybody around wherever he moved. The remaining wizard looked meaningfully at Anybody and asked with all sincerity, "How do things look to you?"

The whole situation was becoming quite unpleasant. Anybody felt it was better not to let it show, but it always seemed to be right there in front of him wherever he would look. The more nervous he became the more the mirror would laugh, until he noticed it wasn't a mirror after all. It was the other wizard, who had the most concerned, warm expression on his face. "Why are you here?" he asked courteously.

The other wizard interrupted before Anybody could answer. "There are reasons, you know, reasons." They both laughed again and slapped each other on the back.

Anybody thought perhaps he had better leave. He asked the way out, but neither wizard answered. They just turned to each other and looked back at Anybody with displeasure. The first wizard took Anybody by the hand. "No, no, you can't leave yet, now can you? You must ask for the help you need first, but not yet. First we wish to share with you a story."

They took Anybody, who begrudgingly agreed to listen mostly out of fear, and they placed him in a chair and handed him a book. They very sincerely told him that this was the book of time. The first wizard said while he held it he would constantly hear the winds of time and change. Anybody became aware of the sound of rushing wind—Shoooooooosssshhh-hhhhh, shoooooooosssshhhhhhhh.

The sound came from his other side—the second wizard was nearby. To-gether now . . . Shoooooooosssshhhhhhhhh, shoooooooooosssshhhhhhhh. The wizards continued to make the sound of the winds of time and change. The second wizard's face was almost beatific, eyes moist and unfocused. Only later did Anybody realize that the first wizard had been speaking in his other ear. And through this rushing torrent of sound he first heard one wizard in one ear say, "There's no need to talk and no need to move." While in the other ear he continued to hear the sounds of the winds of time and change. Then they would reverse and the winds of time and change would rush in the other ear, and in the other ear he heard, "There is no need to listen and no need to hear because now it is time to find a mem-ory from a long time ago."

Now torrents of memories flooded him, washing away well-guarded se-crets. But the voice continued in the other ear. "There's no need to re-member—it's a boring task to remember anything, shoooooooosssshhhh-hhhh, shoooooooosssshhhhhhhh."

But suddenly he was finished before he had even started. He stood there facing the two wizards, who were laughing and slapping each other on the back in an uncontrollable fashion. Anybody shook his head to clear it, but he seemed to be very drowsy and half asleep and half awake and very unsure of which was which.

He opened his eyes and the wizard who was facing him said, "I am very sorry for mistreating you so. Perhaps we were a bit hard on you." The wizard extended his hand in friendship. Anybody reached for it automatically. The next thing he was aware of was picking himself up off the street; his clothes were dry and the sun was coming up.

He had lost hours and he had no idea where to look to find them. He only got halfway up, however, before he realized that he had been lying on a large book, with an inscription on the outside that could not be read. "The diary, how did I find it?" He grabbed it and ran back to his guest house.

He packed his things and paused only to debate whether to hide the book or quickly try to rush it back to the sorcerer and sorceress. Then he stopped all together and curiosity began to gnaw at him. He asked, "What was written in this book?" He decided he should read it and make sure it was the right book, even though it was the only one left.

He turned to the first page, and though he continually blinked hard, a large hand reached right out of the first page and grabbed him by the collar and dragged him back into the book.

This may sound somewhat strange to you, but this was a somewhat strange book. Anybody couldn't believe it either. Anyway, the person on the end of the hand was very large. He looked down at Anybody, who was watching him, and inquired, "So you want to learn something, do you?"

Anybody was quite terrified at this and he assured the person that he did not want anything. "This whole thing is just a coincidence, an accident," Anybody insisted.

The giant figure leaned over him and deviously stated, "I know, this is earth coincidence control center. And what exactly don't you want to learn?"

Anybody insisted that he didn't want to learn anything except how to get out of the book. The figure only replied, "I know, and so you must go over there and empty that pail." The figure pointed to a large bucket near Anybody.

Anybody approached the bucket and looked in but there was nothing in the bucket, and became very confused and his head began to spin trying to figure out what this meant. He looked up to say there was nothing in the bucket but there was no one in the room, just him, in his room with a closed book.

Time seemed to stand still. The next thing he heard was the Sorcerer's voice. ". . . gaps in your experience . . . and remember well that today's 'is' was yesterday's 'will be' at the same time that it will be tomorrow's . . ."

Time was up; therefore it was high time that Anybody bestirred himself from the present past memories. In no time, he slipped into an alley that led him to a point to the door. Oooops. He continued on his way down the street, pausing to catch his breath. "I must continue," he thought to himself.

He pushed on to the next likely site. He went up by the stepping stones near the door, and there on the door was a sign that read, "Opening this door is a moving experience." Anybody hesitated. He wished to find the diary but was in no hurry to meet the absurd. But he followed the stepping stones in. And as he did he thought to himself, "This is a crying shame. I have no idea where to look." But through the tears he received an answer.

"Look in the deep freeze." Anybody jumped back. He was getting quite unnerved by all this. He went down a flight of stairs and on the fourth step down he took flight. "Oh no, not again." He thought back to his shattering experience before. He was quite relieved to find that he held himself together long enough to reach the bottom of the stairs. Placing his foot on the floor he heard a loud scream. "Yhaaaaaaaaaa, yhaaaaaaaaaaaaa!"

Anybody jumped with surprise.

"Be careful," a voice scolded him.

"Of what?" he insisted. He was not going to be pushed around so easily this time.

"Of sore spots," the voice persisted.

Anybody did not know what to think of this, so he ignored the voice and went on his way. He reached a door. A sign hung plainly on the door that read, "Fool's Entrance." Anybody hesitated for a moment and then, swallowing his pride (which by the way did get stuck in his craw), he went in and tried to get back out but he could find no way to get a handle on the door. It just disappeared.

He was floating in a hazy mist. He would get a glimpse of a wagging tongue and hear irritating words; the whole thing in fact was a very bitter experience. He ran into a questioning brow who demanded to know how he had lost face, but Anybody could be of no assistance. Anybody decided that nothing of any value could be kept in this room, so he decided he would start from scratch because nobody knows how many buildings the diary might be in. He saw only one stumbling block between himself and the window. He climbed over it, apologizing as he did so.

He grasped the window sill and to his dismay his head started to swim. He became very dizzy. He thought, "If I could just put my finger on what is making all this happen perhaps I could get my head squarely on my shoulders." With this he stepped on another sore spot and began to spout obscenities. A few fleeting moments passed by, and if all this were not enough, thorns in his side made matters even worse. Anybody was certainly letting the whole thing get way out of hand, so he scraped himself together and slid out of the window into the street.

Anybody fell down with a thump and his thoughts swirled around him. He considered how easy it would be to just pass out, but the urgency of his mission kept him awake. Slowly he opened his eyes, rose to his feet, and in spite of the fact that his head was still swimming, he moved cautiously down the street. After some fruitless exploring, he came to another high building, but this one had a sign on the front of it that said, "Hall of Records." Anybody was taken by this, as he had never heard a sign talk. However, after his initial shock, he entered figuring if he couldn't find the diary at least he could learn something the Sorceress could use to defend the mountain.

As he passed through the front archway, he was taken by an enormous room, the walls of which were lined with huge books. Anybody let his eyes move from wall to wall, volume to volume, reading each title in succession. "The Battle of Beliefs," "Early Emperors," "Family Deaths."

Suddenly Anybody's eyes darted across the room and landed on a leather-bound volume laid separate from the rest entitled, "Particulars." "Ahhh," Anybody said to himself, feeling a bit triumphant. "This must be information of great significance."

Bounding across the room he caught up with the book and opened it to the first page. It was, of course, blank. He turned to the second page and it was blanker than the first. He turned each succeeding page with a deeper and deeper sense of disappointment, as each page was again and again blank. Finally in desperation he screamed, "Where are the particulars?!"

Expecting only the echo of his own voice, you can imagine how surprised Anybody felt when a voice answered, "Why, we are all around you."

Anybody did not understand all this, so he decided it was time to take the book and the Princess and return to the mountain and the Lady. He tucked the diary under his shirt and went to the Princess. Anybody told her of his mission and she agreed to run away with him, but when they reached the walls of the city, soldiers were everywhere, for miles and miles, nothing but armies upon armies.

A small group of officers was just below Anybody and he overheard them while they overlooked him. "We will crush the mountain and the Sorceress in three days, I say," one soldier boasted. Another retorted, "He'll do it in two days, I say. And we won't even have to lift a finger." They all laughed and talked of torture and looting of the mountain.

Anybody knew the end was near. Since he did not have time, he was still back on the mountain, he would have to act, but what could he do alone against the Master and the mighty armies? He was alone with just the Princess, who was looking at the armies and wondering what they would do.

Suddenly and unexpectedly he heard a great wail come up from the center of the castle. It shook the ground so hard that armies fell to their knees again.

"Where's my diary? What thief had defiled my city, my privacy, my diary? DEATH TO ANYBODY WHO IS INVOLVED!"

This quite concerned Anybody, who thought that for sure he had been discovered. But he had already made up his mind; he would have to face the Master anyway or the mountain would be lost, and it would be too hard for him to lose a mountain.

He drew himself up. "Who screams for Anybody screams for me," Anybody replied in a loud voice. Anybody handed the diary to the Princess and told her that she was to try to bring it to the Lady of the mountain, if she could do it in time.

He turned from her and walked out into the plaza at the main gate. There stood the Master of the Unknown, hatred burning in his heart, steel gleaming in his eyes, death written all over his face.

"So, you are a little spy and a thief?" the Master bellowed.

"Can you raise your voice another foot?" Anybody requested quickly. This unbalanced the Master, who only expected to crush an ant.

"Where is it?" the Master demanded. His eyes poured over Anybody, who stood watching him.

Anybody was ready for death. His mind was cracking with the strain as the Master searched through his thoughts. Anybody could not stand the pressure. "I gave it to the Princess, she has it." Anybody could not believe he had divulged the secret. He looked up at the Master.

The Master gazed at him keenly. "Do you think I am such a fool as that? Now, where is it really?"

Anybody was dumbfounded by this. He had no reply but silence.

The Master's anger grew. He grabbed Anybody and threw him down at his feet. "I know no one would give such a prize to a naive girl. Now, where is it?"

Anybody realized by listening intently that opportunity was calling. The Master would not kill him without learning the location of the diary and the Master would not believe the location of the diary. Anybody began to laugh and laugh. The Master struck him silent.

The Master threw a sly glance at Anybody, raising his hands in the air. The sun waned. Day turned to night. Moonlight struck Anybody as he stood up, very surprised to find himself in the Lady's garden on the mountain.

He turned around and around in disbelief, but sure enough he was there. The Sorceress came out of the trees and smiled at him. "You had a close call, but we have saved you, our little warrior." Anybody could still not believe he was saved. "How did I get here?"

The Lady smiled and turned back to the trees. The Sorcerer came out in the moonlight. His robes glistened and his voice reassured Anybody. "I could not let you be destroyed, after all you have done in our behalf."

Anybody said, "But how did you do it?"

The Sorcerer replied, "We have many powers even the Master of the Unknown does not understand." The Sorcerer placed his arm on Anybody's back, comforting him. "But now, my little friend, before we eat and drink together, you must tell us where the diary is because Time is short."

Anybody became somewhat confused by this. His recollection had been that Time was quite tall. This suggested a way to test this reality. Anybody replied, "How tall is Time?"

The Sorcerer looked confused. "We do not have time for games."

Anybody replied, "I do not want to play. I just want to know his height and I will tell you where."

The Sorcerer was becoming impatient. "Time tall, how tall, stop this nonsense. War is at hand, the diary, the diary!"

Anybody began to laugh but was awakened by Blink, only to find all the wise men of the forest were still discussing his problem. One of the wise men turned to Anybody, who was still shaking off his sleep and dreams. "Did you have a nice rest?"

Anybody was confused but in the interest of politeness replied, "Why, yes I did, but I had the most peculiar dreams."

The wise man turned back to the others. "He is awake now. We can begin the inquiry."

Anybody asked, "What inquiry?"

The wise man condescendingly replied, "You wish to have a solution to your problem. We have agreed to help, but we must have some data."

Anybody could understand this, so he agreed to answer any questions they thought might help.

The oldest-looking of the wise men began, "Do you have any personal property?"

Anybody shook his head, "No." Then he remembered, "Well, I have my clothes, at least I think they're mine."

The old wise man looked at Anybody closely. "No rings, books, etc. . ."

Anybody had to reply, "No."

The second wise man asked if he could recall anything of importance at all. Again Anybody had to reply "no." The next wise man asked him if he remembered anything from his dreams, anything symbolic like hiding something that might be a key to his identity.

Anybody thought for a moment and then, smiling slightly, he said, "There was something . . ."

"What was that?" All the wise men leaned forward looking expectantly.

Anybody also leaned forward, looking at them intently. "You're right—there was something I hid, but this is not now." The wise men looked confused at Anybody, who was watching them closely. "What?" they all said in unison.

Anybody repeated himself. "This is not now, is it? . . . Do you SEE WHAT I'M SAYING?"

The wise men looked up and left. The Master of the Unknown stood before him. Anybody looked at the Master of the Unknown, whose anger and desperation had grown by enormous proportions. Anybody inquired of him, "Do you really want your diary so badly?"

The Master replied, "It is my personal property. I will squash you and skin you and burn you in oil."

Anybody was unimpressed. "Do you want it badly enough to gamble for it?"

The Master looked at Anybody suspiciously. "Gamble?" The Master said to himself, "I will gamble. At what game?"

Anybody replied, "You are supposed to be the wisest man in all the land, in fact, the wisest of all. I will ask you a question. If you answer it I give you the diary. If you fail, I get my freedom. Will you take an oath, by spell on your life?"

The Master was desperate, so he agreed to the gamble and the oath.

Anybody looked up at the Master to himself. He stalled for a few moments.

The Master grew impatient. "Let us begin, ask away."

Anybody took a deep breath, savoring the moment and licking his lips. "What is the name that your parents called you as a child?"

The Master gasped. He was trapped between defeat and death. He murmured, "Ralphie."

Anybody screamed in delight. "Ralphie, Ralphie, Ralphie, you're late for dinner. Ralphie, wash your hands and pick up your room!" Anybody went on and on.

The Master grew smaller and younger and younger until he was just a little child. Anybody picked him up and took him to the Princess to be cared for.

Within a few days the armies were disbanded and sent home to their wives and mothers. All the slaves were freed and the great wealth of the Master's city was divided among the poor. Anybody took a small house in a recent oasis in the local desert, married the Princess and used his powers of sorcery to become a great healer of men.

Famine and disease were ended for miles around. The Lady of the mountain gave gifts of plants and herbs to Anybody, who spent his time roaming around healing the poor and needy, trying to do some small good in a vile world.

On his eighty-fourth birthday, a messenger arrived at his house in the oasis. A rather withered princess handed the message to Anybody. It read, "Your help is urgently needed. Please come to the Northern Kingdom at once." Anybody was too old to travel and his memory was failing, so he ignored or forgot it.

Another message came that he treated the same way. Finally, after a third annoyance, Anybody made the journey north, expecting a great plague or massive battle victims. But he found only an over-worried king, who begged him, "Please cure my son."

Anybody, who had by this time come to be regarded as the greatest of sorcerers, looked down at the bed-ridden prince and smiled a queer smile. Slowly he began to speak. "My dear king, I do not have to cure your son, the prince, because your son has no problem at all. In fact, there is no prince at all. All this is just a part of a dream someone is having somewhere who does not know he is really dreaming, and a problem in a dream is no real problem at all. In fact this is no real dream at all; this *is just a fable, and a fable is just one way to let your imagination run away with you now."*